THE RETURN
OF
THE
MATADOR

THE RETURN OF THE MATADOR

by

Astrid Ryterband

www.lulu.com

Lulu Entreprises, Inc.

3101 Hillsborough St.

Raleigh, N.C. 27607

United States

Second Edition – 08/2011

aryterband@yahoo.com

ISBN 978-1-257-80128-2

Author: Ryterband, Astrid Cover Design: Walsh, Valerie

Editor: de Plessy deplessy@yahoo.com

THE RETURN OF THE MATADOR

Summary: *The most famous matador in Spain dies but returns to life as a bull.*

Manufactured in the United States of America

For the Bulls

THE RETURN OF THE MATADOR

By

ASTRID RYTERBAND

Table of Contents

THE RETURN OF THE MATADOR

Prologue

It is siesta, and you must sleep, Rosa.

But Grandmother, first tell me the story of Juan.

Again?

Yes, please.

If I tell it to you again, will you sleep?

Yes, Grandmother. Can I ask you a question?

Yes.

How do you remember everything? You were only twelve.

If something is important to you, you will remember, if not, you will forget.

I won't forget your story.

I know you won't, Rosa, and when you're a grandmother, you can tell it to your grandchildren, too. Ready?

Yes, I am ready. Tell it to me again.

THE BULLFIGHT

Chapter 1

Seville's *La Maestranza* bullring glittered like a white and yellow jewel box in the sand. Antonio and Inez Elmontez, my parents, sat in the bleachers, but not me, I was in the *chiqueros.*

I knew that my grandfather, Juan, was supposed to be the greatest matador in Spain, that he was some kind of hero, but instead of feeling proud, I felt nervous, twisting my long braid. In the dim light of the pen, I recognized the bull from Uncle Pedro's ranch in Arcos de la Frontera. "El Fuerte," I whispered. "Do you remember me?"

El Fuerte snorted and shook his head. "El Fuerte, can I tell you something my Grandmother Rosalita told me?"

The bull blinked his eyes. "El Fuerte, when my mother carried me in her belly, my grandmother made a tiny matador's costume for me. My whole family wanted me to be a boy, so when I arrived they were disappointed."

El Fuerte snorted.

"El Fuerte, I know you don't understand why I can't free you from here."

El Fuerte shook his head and twitched his nostrils, reminding me of the day the little bull was born; he had already begun making his signature gesture back then. I remembered watching El Fuerte sleep next to his mother that first night, his stomach full after enjoying his mother's milk. Now, this beautiful bull was to reach the end of his life. "El Fuerte, I can't believe it's going to end like this."

"And what do you think you're doing here, young lady?" a *picador,* dressed in costume, said, startling me from behind.

I stood in front of the door with my arms spread apart. "No!" I said, sniffing away tears. "I won't let you take El Fuerte. He's my friend."

The picador laughed. "Come on *senorita*, let's take you up to your *madre*." The *picador* outstretched his hand and led me away. "No, let me go…"

Fifteen minutes later, El Fuerte entered the ring, the sun blinding him.

I now sat between my father and mother. We watched my grandfather's every move. I heard my father, Antonio whisper, "Inez, remember how Father taught me to *torear* in *las novilladas?* Watch how he moves the cape just out of reach, dominating the bull."

My mother, Inez nodded, squeezing my hand. We watched the spectacle in the bullring. At first El Fuerte wouldn't charge, so my grandfather, Juan, teased the bull by making passes on his knees, by biting the bull's horns, and the crowd roared its approval. I glanced at father who cheered and whistled. Now, grandfather stepped into the line of charge to persuade El Fuerte to turn. He guided the horns with the center of the *muleta*.

"Soon I will become a superstar like him," Antonio whispered. Then he and the raucous crowd whistled and cheered my grandfather in the bullring who held his ground between passes, linking them in a series of four and five.

I cringed, for I knew what was coming. I watched my grandfather stepping close to El Fuerte, luring him to the center of his cape again and again. The moment of truth had arrived. Grandfather raised his sword to his side.

"No, no!" I screamed, standing up. "Don't kill El Fuerte!"

The bull didn't move, saliva now dripping from his mouth. A whistle came from the stands, then bull and matador both charged and Juan's sword, in a single thrust, plunged two feet into the black mass.

The crowd leaped to its feet. El Fuerte fell onto his hind legs, still thrashing with his horns at the other *toreros* as they gathered around waving their cloaks in his face, until a man with a knife stabbed him in the back of the neck.

Juan stood over the dead bull, then saluted the crowd. With another cheer, the place turned white as people pulled out their handkerchiefs and waved them at the president, while the men in red appeared with horses and dragged the bull's corpse away, leaving a red streak in the sand.

The whistling and handkerchiefs from the crowd in the bleachers fluttered and the president lifted his handkerchief twice to grant two ears of the bull to grandfather as a trophy of his last kill. My mother tried to comfort me.

That's terrible, Grandmother. Then what happened?

VICTORY

Chapter 2

Several moments later, the people went wild. Lifting grandfather onto their shoulders, we tried to follow him. I watched them carry their national hero toward the orange trees of the usually hushed promenade of the Torre del Oro, built as a fortress around 1220. "Juan Elmontez, Juan Elmontez, *victoria, victoria, victoria..!*" Television cameras and paparazzi followed the crowd that rushed across Seville's alleyways like a building wave. The joyous faces and waving arms of women and men overflowed the streets.

Now, the crowd moved north, a force of joyous revelers, filling the tiled streets of the Barrio Santa Cruz. Its balconies, made of intricate, black wrought-iron grillwork were festooned with swirls of crepe paper and clusters of balloons that bobbed against Juan's head as he floated along on the crowd's shoulders.

The crowd filled the *tapas* bars, dragging their matador with it. "*Gracias*," Juan shouted, accepting wine glasses filled with robust *rojos* from Cadiz and Huelva, sherry from Jerez, and glass after glass of Seville's finest home-made *sangria. "Gracias,"* he laughed, taking plates piled high with cured meat with cheese from Valle de los Pedroches, grilled mushrooms and sardines served with plump green olives and asparagus and artichokes from Penaflor.

"*Toma mas, mas,* Juan Elmontez!" a fan shouted, laughing, watching the matador drinking, then swallowing a plateful of food. Juan rolled his eyes. Drinking all this wine had finally affected him. Images of the bar were swirling about him: the bartenders, the paparazzi, the celebrating fans. Now Juan's eyes fixated upon the melting fat that dripped into paper funnels from the hanging hunks of ham.

The crowd moved back outside where guitarists played the impassioned chords of flamenco, and people clapped, sang and stamped to the rhythms, inspired by the joy that one of their own was among them, that they were at this very moment a part of Spain's furious history of brilliantly colored strokes, painted onto the canvas of the world.

Who could have predicted that by tomorrow at this time, the most famous matador in Spain's history would meet his death on a quiet street in Seville? That night, we left the star to his fans, and my mother, father and I walked home.

ADIOS

Chapter 3

In the shade of Parque de Maria Luisa, situated in the heart of Seville's verdant southern end, Juan and I sat together. "How could you do, it, Grandfather, how could you kill El Fuerte, such a lovely bull?" I remember asking him, glancing at a beautiful white dove who stood directly above us.

Juan, who was suffering from a headache, groaned. "Lucita, I did nothing wrong. I've made Spain proud. I've killed bulls; they have a hero, simple as that."

Now walking amidst a pathway of flowerbeds, I said, "But how would you feel being killed like that, humiliated in front of thousands of people who cheer when you fall?"

Walking out of the park, we found ourselves standing in the shadow of the Giralda Tower. The dove was following us, flying from tree to tree. "Lucita, bullfighting is an art. It requires enormous skill and daring, and your *abuelo* has had all that. But now it's over," Juan sighed, and I thought he felt sad that he had agreed to fight his last bullfight yesterday. Then he said, "What am I supposed to do with the rest of my life, watch my son become the rising star?"

Walking along the Barrio Santa Cruz, shopkeepers were still cleaning up from last night's festivities. Now the dove flew from balcony to balcony, keeping a close watch on us. Juan readjusted his sunglasses and blue cap, for today he craved anonymity. His headache prevented him from feeling like a superstar, plus every part of his body ached.

Almost home, we stopped in front of a portal where a vendor's cart stood. Directly above us on the narrow ledge of a balcony, I saw a striped tabby cat step between some potted palms and yesterday's decorative displays of orange and green crepe paper. The dove had landed close to him and the cat hunched down into a hunting position.

"It's wrong, Grandfather, and I can't believe my father is going to do exactly what you've been doing," I said, watching the bird and the cat directly above us.

"*Dos naranjas, por favor*," Juan ordered from the vendor, trying to ignore my last statement.

"Oh, well, that's the difference between girls and boys," he sighed. "Men want action, women want peace and quiet. Is that my fault?"

My eye caught the sight of the tabby cat who had now moved away from the ledge. He sprang upward, leaping toward the dove who was perched atop the balcony's black grillwork. Now, the cat, catching his paw between the paper and a potted palm, struggled to free himself from the paper.

'Grandfather," I cried out, but within a second the cat had pushed his back paws onto another potted palm, sending it careening downward. "Grandfather," I shouted, and the big, potted plant struck my grandfather on the head. He fell!

I knelt beside him on the sidewalk, "Grandfather, Grandfather, wake up, please!"

I traced grandfather's eyebrows with my fingertip. "Juan, can you hear me?"

Juan opened his eyes. He saw my face hovering overhead. The dove had landed on my shoulder, but I didn't notice her. Sirens wailed. "Juan, speak to me, please."

My voice must have sounded like a distant angel to him, floating above the breeze of the Guadalquivir River. Then the dove landed beside Juan. Suddenly, Juan heard a voice, maybe that of a great spirit and he echoed its words, "Juan Elmontez, you are about to pass from this life."

Then Juan bolted into a sitting position, gasping, "No, no…"

"Grandfather, what did you just say? Don't worry, you will not die, now lie down, save your strength." I laid his head down, readjusting his blue cap, hearing the sound of wailing ambulances nearing. The dove landed on Juan's head.

The spirit continued and Juan repeated what he heard, "You, Juan Elmontez, will have another chance to return to this earth and redeem yourself." Grandfather smiled and nodded, trying to resist the comforting arms of death, then he jerked back upright, thrashing and writhing. "No! No!" He opened his eyes and grabbed my wrists, "Help me, Lucita, for I will return…" His grip on my wrist went limp. The greatest bullfighter in all of Spain exhaled and lay still.

I sobbed on grandfather's chest, noticing the paramedics getting out of the ambulance. The dove landed on my shoulder, and then I fainted.

*　　　*　　　*

A moment later, I awoke and saw the dove perched atop grandfather's head, whispering in his ear. Then I felt a ripple of power surging through my grandfather, throwing me off his body. A bull loomed above me, looked about, then galloped down the street. "A bull!" I cried out, stepping onto my feet.

"A bull is loose on the street!" people shrieked, chasing after him. "Look, he is wearing a blue cap. And sunglasses!"

"It's you, Grandfather!" I pointed. I turned toward a bystander who was walking by. "It's him, I tell you, it's him, that bull is my grandfather!" The bystander shrugged his shoulders and chased after the bull.

Still lying on the pavement, the paramedics attempted to revive my grandfather's body with oxygen, and a defibrillator pressed over his heart. Then they lifted him onto a stretcher and placed him inside the ambulance. It raced off to the hospital.

BACK TO LIFE

Chapter 4

That night, while the mystery bull lay in his pen, all of Seville mourned the fate of the most famous matador in all of Spain, Juan Elmontez. How ironic that someone who had fought bulls so bravely for so long, was suddenly rendered powerless within seconds by a little cat, no less?

Stealing away from home, I went to see the mystery bull who was imprisoned at my uncle's ranch. "Hello, beautiful bull," I whispered.

The bull immediately got onto his hooves. He watched me pick up the blue cap, which lay in the corner. "This is your cap, isn't it, Grandfather?" The bull snorted and stamped his hoof. I got closer. "If I put your cap back on your head, you will not gore me, will you?" The bull snorted and shook his head. Then he lowered his head so I could place the blue cap between his horns. I gasped. "Grandfather, nod your head if you truly are Juan, my grandfather, the most famous matador in all of Spain."

The bull nodded his head and I threw my arms around his neck, laughing. "Grandfather, you're alive. You are Juan Elmontez, living in a bull's body."

"Lucita!" From outside, my father called to me.

"I must leave, Father will be angry with me." A moment later, father stood in the doorway. "Lucita, come with me immediately, and leave that bull alone!"

"Yes, Father, but the bull is your father, look at him, talk to him, just please talk to him, you'll see—"

Antonio grabbed me and pulled me away. "That's enough, *vamanos!*"

"Father, you must believe me, just let me prove it to—"

I snuck away later that night. I watched Juan, the bull, in his pen, brooding over his impossible predicament. Yesterday he was the greatest matador in Spain, he killed his last bull and celebrated in the streets, he was a hero. But today he was a bull, the very animal he had sought to conquer for most of his life.

Was all this a miracle, or God's way of punishing him for killing hundreds of bulls?

Juan opened his mouth and tried to form the word, *"Sorry,"* with his tongue, but all that emerged from his mouth was a loud snort that hurt his own ears.

"Grandfather, you have to come to our house to see me because I know the truth. Tomorrow they are going to test you to see how aggressively you will perform in the bullring. You know you will either have to confront a matador or become someone's dinner. We must plan some tricks, after all, who knows more tricks than you, the most famous matador in all of Spain?"

The bull nodded his head, motioning for me to go home. I knew he would come to find me.

HELP ME, LUCITA

Chapter 5

It was nighttime in the Elmontez home. A doctor was in my room, administering a sedative to calm me. My great grandmother, Rosalita was sitting with me, and the dove, which I named, "*Amor,*" was perched outside my window.

Antonio and Inez sat across from each other in the dining salon, waiting for the doctor to emerge. I heard my parents speak. "I guess father's death is too much for her," Antonio said.

"Yes, she should have never gone to the park with him," Inez agreed.

Doctor Villanueva closed my door and crossed the hall. "Keep her quiet for a few days."

My parents rose to their feet. "Thank you, doctor. We'll try to do that," Inez said. "Let me walk you to the door."

The next day, Juan, the bull, was tested to determine how good a fighter he was. Juan knew from his former life as a matador that many questions are asked before a bull enters the ring. Will the bull demonstrate bravery or cowardice under such intense suffering? When the *banderilleros* flash past him to plant their harpoon-tipped sticks into his withers, will he continue to charge, undaunted?

Juan knew what he must do. He faced his examiners. He had to impress them. He had to show them what a brave, crazy fighting machine he was. And once they chose him for a bullfight, then he would find a way to escape. And so, Juan charged again and again, each time exhibiting more rage than the last. The ranch hands, breeders and *banderilleros* watched: "This mystery bull is a matador's dream come true," one said.

Another said, "He's a perfect bull, ruthless, cunning, a killing machine!"

Another said, "Yes, he'll make a most memorable afternoon *corrida.*"

As he was led back to his pen, an exhausted Juan overheard his fate: "We'll call this bull, El Fuertisimo! Antonio Elmontez will fight him in Madrid next week. Call him right now."

Juan was stunned. He must have thought my son must fight **me.** If Antonio succeeds in destroying me, he will become a full status matador and his victory will be seen throughout Spain. I would like Antonio to become famous, but I am being forced to defend my life against my own son, a son I trained so well to destroy bulls.

That night, Juan, the bull, crashed out of his wooden stall, and, beneath an orange moon, galloped over the stone bridge where he saw the golden tower of the Alcazar reflected on the Guadalquivir River. He thought of the Muslims who lived in the Alcazar for five centuries. He thought of the Spanish monarchs who also lived there. Didn't Pedro the Cruel, once live there, too, assassinating his guests? Why, I'm no better, Juan thought, I've assassinated my bull guests, too. I was a bad boy, bad, bad, bad!

Now deserted at this late hour, Juan strode past the Alcazar's lush courtyards hidden by thick walls, fountains and foliage. He remembered proposing to Marbelis, his dear wife. He remembered kissing her for the first time, feeling so alive then, trembling with anticipation and love. All that had happened in another lifetime. Back then he was a human, now he was an animal, a pawn for humans to play with.

At last, Juan arrived at our home, once his home, too. He pushed open the black, wrought-iron garden gate and snuck up to my room. My dove*, Amor,* greeted him. A breeze flipped the corner of the handmade lace curtain so that he could see me sleeping in my lace-covered bed. Sitting in the rocking chair was his snoring mother, Rosalita, holding a rosary between her fingers.

Juan poked his muzzle across the window sill, his left horn catching the lace curtain. He tried to say the words, "Lucita, *madre*, it's me…" but only a groan emerged from his mouth. No response. He pushed his head farther inside, rattling the blinds. My eyes opened for a second, then closed once again. This time, Juan walked over to the bedroom door and gave it a shove. It opened. He was inside.

I bolted upright, eyes wide open. I got out of bed and slowly edged toward the bull that snorted and shook his head. I moved even closer toward him. "What's the matter, Grandfather?"

Juan let out a cry which came out louder than he had expected. Now Rosalita cleared her throat and opened her eyes to see a strange vision before her. She removed her glasses, wiped them clean, placed them back onto her nose, but still saw the same vision: a bull was standing before her. Rosalita shrugged her shoulders and fell back asleep.

Just then, I heard footsteps nearing. "Grandfather, go out, quickly, they're coming."

My father stepped into my bedroom. "How are you feeling, Lucita? Please, go back to bed, I have some excellent news to tell you."

I got back in bed and sat up. "Yes, Father, what is it?"

Antonio sat at the edge of my bed. "Well, on Sunday I will fight in the first professional bullfight of my career."

"That's too bad, father. I hate that."

"Now, Lucita don't forget your family's tradition. We are matadors, plain and simple. I've worked hard to reach this point in my career. My father would have been proud of me."

"Your father is a bull now. You know that, I told you many times."

"Stop it, Lucita. Stop uttering that nonsense. I've simply come to inform you that the mystery bull we found running in the streets the day your grandfather died is the bull I will kill in Madrid on Sunday."

I let out a horrific scream. I wouldn't stop. Antonio backed away, frightened by my violent reaction to his good news. This time, Rosalita awoke. "Lucita, stop screaming, you'll have me lose my hearing once and for all. Antonio, leave at once, you have a habit of upsetting your daughter.

Go, go, go!" she shouted, using her bony frame to push father out of the room.

Several moments later, the bull pushed the bedroom door open again, snorting at Rosalita. The old woman froze, blinking furiously. I said, "Rosalita, it's your son, touch him, he won't hurt you."

From the corner of one eye, Rosalita glared at me. "Please believe me, I promise you that this is your son, Juan. He died and returned as a bull. It's true, it's really, really true, just touch him. Just once."

Rosalita stepped up to the bull and put her face up to his muzzle. Juan blinked. Dumbfounded, Rosalita then wrapped her hands around the bull's horns. Juan stood passively. Now Rosalita beat her knuckles on the bull's face, between his horns.

"You see? He has no intention of harming you, do you, Juan?"

Juan shook his head. Rosalita gasped, "How can this be true, Lucy? Tell me."

I described her son's last afternoon, emphasizing the exact moment when Juan the man died and Juan, the bull appeared.

Rosalita touched her rosary and prayed, "Dear God, give us strength, for we have a difficult road ahead of us. I must convince our family that a miracle has occurred."

She turned to the bull, wrapping her arms around his neck. "*M'ijo,* Juanito, is it really you? How does it feel to be a bull instead of a man, you crazy boy?"

Juan tried to shrug his shoulders, as he had done for decades when he was a man, but this time it had no effect, so he shook his head again, unable to reply. Rosalita began to weep, "Juanito, Juanito, my son, you're here, you're here, don't worry, we'll get you out of this situation. But how?" She turned to me. "How?"

I sat near the bull and patted his head. "I have an idea. Father won't like it, yet we have no choice. This is it. Are you listening, Grandfather? "

This time Juan nodded his head. His fate was in my hands, that of a wise girl he should have listened to a long time ago.

ANTONIO'S PRAYER

Chapter 6

It was the Saturday night before the Sunday of Antonio's debut bullfight in Madrid. I was strolling in downtown Seville with my friends. I saw my father walking down a quiet street, passing his favorite pubs. One was called *El Burladero,* an old Ernest Hemingway bar, decorated with bullfighting memorabilia. Antonio was about to enter the old Hemingway bar, but decided to visit Juan Ramon's *Garlochi Bar* in the medieval Plaza de la Alfalfa instead.

After Antonio entered, we gazed through the window. I watched my father nodding at Juan Ramon, the deeply religious, ardent collector of church artifacts, who sat alone, contemplating a statue of Jesus Christ. Antonio walked up to the bar's counter, adorned with vases of exotic flowers. He ordered his favorite drink, Ramon's house specialty, a potent drink called, '*Sangre de Cristo*.' The somber bust of Christ gazed upon him.

Sitting among lighted altar candles and smoking pots of church incense, Antonio prayed for strength, for courage and for support in his coming ordeal in Madrid. He took a few sips of the drink, nodded at Ramon and left.

I followed my father walking through the ancient labyrinthe quarter inhabited by the Jews prior to their expulsion from Spain in 1492. I remembered how we liked to walk in these little winding alleys off the Plaza Santa Maria La Blanca. The scent of flowers from the Murillo Gardens, the Baroque churches, the cafes and tapas bars would usually cheer him, but today I knew that nothing could ease the pressure weighing him down. He entered the house, and I went inside the house through my room.

THE ARGUMENT

Chapter 7

I was sitting on my parent's bed, watching them pack their belongings for their trip to Madrid in the morning. "Mother, please, make him believe me, please, he's just got to believe me, he can't fight Juan tomorrow, Juan is his father, he's come back to life as a bull, so, father, you just can't stick a sword into his heart—"

"Stop it, Lucita, right now!" father bellowed. I fought to hold my tears. This was the first time I had ever heard father shout at me.

"Lucita, go into your room and prepare a suitcase for tomorrow," mother ordered.

"No, I will not. I will prove to you that the bull you plan on fighting is no ordinary bull. That bull is your father, my grandfather, and the least you can do is talk to him, Father."

"Talk to him, talk to him. Lucita, don't you hear yourself, you're twelve years old, you know better than to believe you can talk to an animal, a bull no less."

"You put only one sock in your suitcase, father. Where's the second sock?"

"What?"

My mother and I smiled for a moment, realizing how upset Antonio was. "Oh." Antonio picked up his second sock and placed it with its mate inside his suitcase. "All this strange talking about your grandfather is costing me my rest. I haven't slept in days, how do you expect me to fight my very first *corrida* with no sleep, just tell me that, Lucita?"

"That's just it; your conscience is telling you that you're wrong."

"Don't tell me about my conscience, *senorita.* I'm the man here, I'm the father, I'm the head of this house and I am ordering you to stop talking about the bloody bull. Don't you understand there's no backing down now? Hundreds of people are counting on me, my career, my reputation, our good name is on the line now, and I will indeed fight this mystery bull you call Juan, whom you say is my father, for I don't care if he's my uncle, my brother, or my cousin, whomever the bull is, I don't give a damn because I **am** going to sword him, and yes, I **am** going to k –"

"No, no, no, no…" I shrieked, holding my hands to my ears.

"Antonio, why do you make Lucita cry?" Mother ran after me.

SAVING JUAN

Chapter 8

Early the next morning, Antonio and Inez left for Madrid. As soon as they left, my great grandmother, Rosalita and I, got into our car and sped off for Uncle Reynaldo's ranch in Cremona, in the outskirts of Seville. Reynaldo, Antonio's brother, lived with another brother, Uncle Pedro and his family. When we arrived, Juan, the bull was gone.

Reynaldo said, "They came for the bull earlier than they said they would, they're off to Madrid!"

"Oh, no, what should we do?" I wailed.

"*Vamanos*, everybody in the truck!" Rosalita, Reynaldo, his brother, Pedro, his wife, Carmen, their five year old son, Francisco, and I, immediately piled into an old pick-up truck and sped off, hoping to catch up to Juan.

"We can't let them kill Juan, we just can't," I said.

"Don't worry, Lucita, the bull won't gore your father," Francisco said.

"Oh, you're only five years old, Francisco. It's not my father I'm worried about; it's the bull, the bull. The bull is my grandfather."

"What? Are you crazy? That's impossible!" the five year old said.

"You'll soon see, Francisco, that's a promise."

The pick up truck passed seas of wheat and row after row of brilliant sunflowers. Hours later, we drove onto the Despennaperros Mountain Pass which at last, in the distance to the north, would lead to the mountains of Toledo and the outline of the Tagus. Another two hours passed. We found ourselves on the empty highway in the outskirts of Toledo. "Look! Up ahead, it's the truck, it's the truck!" Carmen Elmontez gestured. Reynaldo passed the truck which was transporting Juan, the bull.

"Why did you pass him, Uncle, go back!" I said.

"You'll see, I have a plan. This is the plan…you must all lie still in the middle of the road…as though there has been a terrible accident…"

Moments later, the entire family got out of the truck surrounding me. I lay in the middle of the road, feigning injury. Reynaldo, a former actor, shrieked and waved his arms in the hot wind like a tenor in an opera. "Stay down, stay down…" The others looked at one other. They knew Uncle Reynaldo was a little *loco*, that he was prone to manic fits of dramatic emotion, but did they, too, need to behave this way?

"Do as I do, everybody, my plan will work, but do this or the driver won't stop."

Reluctantly, the Elmontez family emulated Uncle Reynaldo's flamboyant gestures. Now the truck carrying Juan came into view from the bottom of the hill. The driver, whistling, saw the sight before him, his eyes narrowing. He glanced at his watch: he still had plenty of time to get to Madrid with the bulls, so he slowed to a stop at the side of the road and got out, stepping toward the group stretched out in the middle of the road.

"I broke my leg, *senor*," I cried.

"Did you have an accident?" the driver asked.

Everyone sobbed simultaneously, except for Reynaldo who inched away from the scene, sneaking behind the cattle truck, forcing its rear door open. Out flocked a group of grateful bulls, their hooves landing on the hot cement. They sauntered across the road, found a grove of cork trees and lay down in the shade.

Last of all, a huge, proud bull stepped from the truck. He stopped and looked Reynaldo in the eye. "Is it you, father?" Reynaldo asked.

From the corner of my eye, I saw the bull and Reynaldo facing each other. Then I stood up, to the utter amazement of the driver. "I feel much better now, *senor*, excuse me, please."

"You what?" The driver watched me and my family run toward his truck.

The driver started following us, smelling a rat. "Hey, what's going on here?"

I stood before the bull and our family. "Go ahead, Grandfather," I said to the bull, "show us who you really are. I will put your cap on your head." Slowly, Juan, the bull lowered his head and I placed the cap atop his head. Reynaldo, Pedro, Carmen and Francisco gasped. Their eyes met Rosalita's and saw the truth in her eyes: the bull was truly Juan Elmontez, who had come back to life.

Pedro, Carmen and Francisco bowed before the bull. Reynaldo said, "Juan, my honored *padre* who was once the greatest matador in all of Spain, please allow us to escort you to our truck."

But the driver ran toward us, saw the bulls under the trees and began to curse and shake his fists, lunging toward Reynaldo who shouted, "Hurry, hurry, go to the truck, take the bull!"

"Thieves, criminals, give back my bulls," the driver shouted, hitting Reynaldo in the stomach. They fought there on the side of the road, punching each other. Reynaldo looked at the sky, made a fist, sighed and said,

"Sorry, *amigo*," then cracked the driver across his jaw. The driver landed on his back.

"Sorry, *senor,* nothing personal," Reynaldo said, running back to the truck.

"Hurry, Uncle, hurry…" I said. Reynaldo got into their truck, pressed on the accelerator and turned the truck back into the direction of Seville.

The driver raised his head, rubbed his jaw, and drove off, reaching for his telephone.

But our victory was short lived. An hour later, the police caught up with our truck and took Juan with them. "You're all *locos*," the police officer admonished us. "You claim that this bull is Juan Elmontez returned from the dead?"

"Yes, it's true, officer, just let me prove it to you," I said in tears.

"That won't be necessary, *chica.* Matador or bull, it is not for us to decide. The mayor of Madrid has ordered us to take this bull to his final destination: Madrid. Your father is supposed to fight this bull today and nothing can stop this bull's destiny. Now, kindly move out of the way."

We all exchanged goodbyes with Juan, who climbed into the police truck without a struggle.

Juan stole a look at me. He knew I had done everything in my power to save him from his fate. He saw me sobbing. Then, Rosalita, Francisco, Carmen, Pedro and Reynaldo raised their hands and waved goodbye to him.

MADRID

Chapter 9

Antonio was dressing for the bullfight. His dressers helped him get into his skin-tight *traje de luce* that was red, blue, gold and white, with shiny studs and tassels, taut suspenders, and the false pig's tail that all matadors wear. The dressers left and Antonio knelt down to pray, then he paced up and down. He said aloud, "The kill, of course, is the most difficult moment…you must take your eyes off his horns, guide them down to the *muleta,* then at the same time bury your sword between the bull's shoulder blades…"

Antonio broke out into a cold sweat and whispered, "I can't imagine accomplishing this today. I am afraid, but it is time to go."

The car was waiting to take him to the *corrida.*

THE BULLRING

Chapter 10

That day there was a brass band, three old men with trumpets and drums who announced that the opening parade had begun. Men riding on dancing horses, wore black costumes with scarves, other heavyset men were dressed in red, holding wooden sticks. Hefty *picadores* with pointed spears in leather armor also rode on horses. Then the *toreros* entered with *subalternos and banderilleros.* The stars of the spectacle: are the three *matadors*, - the most experienced *torero* on the left, - the second oldest on the right, - the youngest, my father, Antonio Elmontez, in the middle. They all bowed to the president of the fight, sitting at his balcony in a gray suit, then trooped out into the circle surrounding the sand, protected by thick wooden barricades, the *burladeros.*

I remember that on a lonely highway just outside of Madrid, our family and I bounced and jolted in the truck, driving as fast as we could to stop the *corrida.* Finally, we arrived and stood in a corner, watching.

The first part, the *tercio de varas* began, and Juan, the bull, came racing out of his stall, more than half a ton of thrashing flesh concentrated into two deadly horns rising from its head. There was an "*ah*" from the crowd when the bull rushed out into the sand, the pain of the rosette pinned on his shoulders already angering him. The *subalternos* waved their purple and yellow capes as the bull charged wildly around the arena, the audience assessing him, whistling.

Now the *picadores* appeared on their well padded horses. Two of them came striding and sat in their saddles, waiting for the bull to charge at them. Juan galloped diagonally away from them, but was too slow: one *picador* swiftly thrust his long pike into his shoulder. Juan gasped in agony, then galloped into a corner, trying to breathe deeply, to forget the pain of his deep, bloody wound, and gain energy for the next attack.

Next, the second *picador* rushed in on horseback, pointing his steel-tipped pole at Juan, but this time the bull leaped up and knocked the man out of his saddle.

The spectators howled. They watched the fallen *picador* run for his life, then, to everyone's utter astonishment, the bull crushed the pole with his powerful hooves, took a few broken pieces and chewed them into a mangled mess, spitting out saliva and wood. The people roared in laughter. The TV cameras edged closer to the entertaining bull.

The *banderilleros* entered the ring, frightened, nevertheless aiming their brightly colored, harpoon-pointed *banderillas* at the bull. Now, one *banderillero* ran toward him, but Juan bounced him on the ground. Then the second one came up on Juan's rear, and with a single stroke, just passing within inches of his horns, landed home his red and yellow spear. Applause and whistling rang out and the crowd was excited.

Juan heard great shouts of *ole* come from the onlookers and he shook his head in self-pity and rage.

He chased the *banderilleros* out of the ring, scaring them every step of the way.

And then came a strange silence: everyone stopped cheering. From the back, Antonio watched the bull stare at the entire audience, looking them in the eye. He circled the arena, inching toward the first row of the *barreras.* The bull was thinking, "if only I could speak, I would say to all of you: imagine you people happy to see these knives stuck into my body, blood dripping from my face onto my bloodied shoulders. You don't know how it feels to be out here, humiliated, alone. You have no mercy. I'll pull one of you down here and see how you feel."

The spectators looked at one another, and a hush rose from the bleachers, spreading across the entire bullring like a solemn meeting of the minds. This bull was speaking to them. Some backed into their seats uncomfortably; others hung their heads, while others sobbed.

Maybe I should just let Antonio kill me and end it all, Juan thought. How can I hope to change Spain's tradition? I am just a bull, a stupid, low animal, born to this earth to either amuse people or be eaten by them. I cannot change their minds.

With the hesitant wave of the president's handkerchief, and a bar from the band, the wounded bull was left alone, panting, his tongue hanging from its mouth. Again, he limped in a circle around the entire bullring, staring down everyone who sat in the bleachers. There was dead silence and a hot wind. "What's going on?" people asked.

Antonio, the star performer came striding out, his *muleta* tucked under one arm. He marked the sign of the cross, then he raised his cap, saluting the spectators. He tossed it into the air behind him, and it landed facedown. It would be bad luck for the matador if it landed the other way.

The crowd cheered for the son of their national hero. A trumpet sang out across the bullring. Antonio's silken suit of lights reflected the hot glints of the five o'clock sun. He strutted before the crowd, stealing a glance at my mother, sitting in the first row of seats.

She nodded at him, and he closed his eyes to breathe deeply. When he opened his eyes, he was startled to see that Juan was standing quietly in front of him. His and the bull's eyes locked. Antonio appraised the superb animal, glossy black with horns like crescent moons.

The audience sat at the edge of their seats. "How dare Elmontez allow the bull to come so close to him?" "Isn't he afraid?" "What is going on there?"

Juan, the bull realized: how strange it is to see this ring once again, not as a matador, but as a bull. This time he was not the killer, he was the killer's prey. And the killer was to be his dear, beloved son. Juan stared calmly at my father.

My father decided to wave the *muleta* and go through the first passes. The cheering turned into silence, for now, Juan charged and charged, letting my father display all his matador skills, after all, he didn't want him to be shamed in front of the world. Antonio stood firm, chest out, chin hooked in, his lower lip curled over his upper lip, tempting the bull with flicks of the cape, drawing him in.

There were gasps, howls, cheers, applause, boos and whistles from the agitated crowd.

Then Antonio stopped. He noticed that the bull was panting. It was time for the kill. The matador was handed his *estoque*, from behind the barricade and stood over the exhausted bull ready to strike, enticing it to lower its head once more, opening up the vertebrae for the entry of the blade straight into his lungs. The bull watched his son step toward him, holding the sword horizontally, but suddenly the bull decided to take two steps backward, and the crowd fell silent. No one could remember a bull like this.

Antonio looked into those eyes that looked so much like his father's. He hesitated, and the crowd began yelling at him:

"Coward, coward," they screamed. "Kill him!"

Antonio marched up to the bull, raising his sword for the fatal strike.

It was then that Reynaldo, Pedro, Carmen, Rosalita, Francisco and I ran into the bullring. My dove flew above, leading us. The spectators were astounded. Who would be crazy enough to enter a bullring just before the kill? Inez stood up and gasped, "My daughter!"

I ran right up to my father, positioning myself between him and the bull. Antonio choked and stepped back.

I was stroking the bull and kissing his nose. Antonio watched me smile. "You see, father, he is not a wild beast."

Pandemonium broke out among the spectators of the bullring. Inez jumped off the first row of seats and ran toward me. The spectators moved in toward the front row and the television crew bounced into the ring. We embraced the bull. Now the people climbed into the ring to witness the miracle. Some fainted, some wept and some proclaimed me, a girl of twelve at the time, to be a modern day saint.

I said, "Father, this bull is your father, Juan Elmontez. He came back to life as a bull. Isn't it true, Grandfather?" And Juan, the bull, tenderly licked my face with his big pink tongue.

Antonio and the bull looked into each other's eyes. Antonio hesitated, but this time he couldn't mistake his father's loving gaze. He let out a sob, threw his arms around the bull and cried, "*Father! You are injured, you're bleeding.*" Inez joined her husband and also hugged the bull.

Several veterinarians rushed through the crowd and administered the wounded bull, removing the rosette and blades, treating the wounds and injecting antibiotics through an IV tube. Photographers took photos. People cried and prayed and TV anchor women and men babbled rapidly into their microphones as their camera crew filmed the momentous scene. They all repeated the word, "*milagro.*" Two helicopters flew overhead to film the scene. The miracle of Juan, the bull, spread over the TV cables, making news across Spain.

"Will he survive?" Rosalita asked the doctors. The family conferred with the medical staff in hushed voices and whispers.

"Where will the bull go now? Back to the ranch in Seville?" a reporter asked Antonio.

“Ranch?” Antonio said. “He is my dear father, he will return to the home he has always lived in. With us!”

After at least a half hour, the doctors gave their approval for the bull to return home in an ambulance. The people cheered with relief. They parted to make room for the wounded bull, limping alongside his family.

The people, the photographers, and the TV crew followed us as far as the ambulance. Then, Juan stepped inside a trailer hooked onto the rear of the ambulance, followed by us and several doctors. We waved goodbye to the spectators, but one last question asked by a TV anchor person echoed through the crowd. "What will you do now, Antonio Elmontez? Will you still fight bulls?" And we sped away.

TOWARD SEVILLE

Chapter 11

A half hour later, Madrid was behind us. The ambulance driver drove through the open countryside where olive, cork and fig trees grew. The only people who lived in this countryside were the shepherds who spent their days tending to their sheep.

At the top of the hill, one of these shepherds, a young man of no more than eighteen or nineteen, looked down and saw a white ambulance and trailer driving below. Then the shepherd saw something surprising: from the rear window of the ambulance, someone tossed out a large, scarlet cloth. He watched it blow down the road behind the truck. The ambulance and trailer at last fell out of view, but the cloth lingered, catching itself in a patch of low shrubs beside the road.

In the days that followed, little by little, the wind blew dust and sand onto the red cloth, until only a small patch of color remained. And in the end, the patch, which had become as small as a red petal, vanished from sight.

JUAN'S RETURN

Chapter 12

That is happy and sad all at the same time, Grandmother.

Rosa, you aren't sleeping.

There's a little more to the story, I know there is.

Alright, I'll tell you the true ending, but then you must fall asleep.

Yes, what happened after the cape went out the window?

After my grandfather was hit on the head by the potted plant, the ambulance took us to the hospital where he lay in his deathbed for hours. I became conscious again, ecstatic over the amazing dream I just had. I couldn't wait to tell my family about it.

My grandfather had only a faint pulse, although on a screen we could see much brain activity. Outside the hospital window the citizens of Seville surrounded the hospital, praying for their matador hero to regain consciousness.

Outside the window, my dove, *Amor* sat, watching us very carefully. Even the tabby cat that had caused the accident sat next to *Amor.* After a few minutes, *Amor* flew through the window and sat on Juan's head and whispered the winding path of dreams in his ear.

After a few seconds, my grandfather's eyelids fluttered and he murmured softly, "Never again, never again, never again…" And then his eyes opened to see all of us watching him. He saw me.

"Lucita, Lucita, I must tell you where I've been, you saved my life, and Antonio, there you are, you didn't sword me, you didn't, you couldn't, mother, there you are, my sons…"

I was stunned. He was recounting the very dream I had dreamed! I stared at *Amor* closely. Her eyes lit up when she saw me questioning her. She whispered something to me, but I didn't understand her. Then I turned back to grandfather and we all cheered. The doctors entered, amazed at grandfather's recovery.

"There was a bullfight, in Madrid, then you all stopped Antonio from--, and the cape, it's out there, in the desert, with the shepherd, in the wind, in the dust, it's gone. Forever."

And my tears fell, and we all laughed, and since that day, my grandfather and father never raised their swords again.

Rosa, are you sleeping?

She's sleeping, Lucita. You told the dream well.

Thank you, Amor, my love dove. When I am gone, will you stay with Rosa?

Of course, and I will send her my dreams, too.

THE END

Author's Note

Some readers ask me where I got the idea for *The Return of the Matador*. It came from a saying, "Walk a mile in my shoes." Then my mind danced with memories, with images of my travels in Spain, of its bulls who must fight matadors, yet before the fight they are already programmed to lose to the matadors. I cannot change a country's traditions. I am just one writer. But I can try.

--Astrid Ryterband 2009--

ALSO BY ASTRID RYTERBAND

Children's Fiction

Dennis, the Pigeon of Venice

My Babushkas' Itches

The Sequin Galaxy

The Magic Pencil

Illustrated Humor

Brrreak the T- Addiction

Novellas

Out of the Silents

Novel

An Aria For Her Soul

Theater

Greta D. and the I.R.S.

A Musical in Two Acts

Lyrics, Music, Score & Libretto

www.ingramcontent.com/pod-product-compliance
Ingram Content Group UK Ltd.
Pitfield, Milton Keynes, MK11 3LW, UK
UKHW041923190726
13854UKWH00003B/1402

9 781257 801282